THE SILK DRESS

Shiela Y. Harris

ISBN-13-9780967931296

DEDICATION

Fiction is a literature created from the imagination, not presented as fact, though it may be based on a true story or situation. Types of literature in the fiction genre include the novel, short story, and novella.

As a super fan of the novelist, "Steven King" I think this will peak and hold every reader's interest as I indulge in a broad, everyday usage of a fictional short story which refers to appearance, impression, and understanding that is imaginary or otherwise not strictly true.

Incorporated are actual events used to help build the storyline. This work is dedicated to all my current and new readers.

FORWARD

Shiela Harris again does what she does best as a writer. As she expresses herself with words, the ideas, the information, coupled with research gives her great joy as she allows her mind to wander with thoughts and concepts. This is one of ten books, and to date proves to be very different from previous works but no less intriguing.

TABLE OF CONTENT

THE STORM

Chapter One

While going through antique furnishings, old clothing and other stored items in the attic, Claudia uncovered a cardboard box tied with twine. As she wiped and blew across the top and sides of the box, a small cloud of dust particles burst in the air, highlighted by the sunrays coming through the tiny attic window.

Home was the best place to be during a massive winter storm in Kansas City. The storm spanned 20 states dumping more than a foot of snow as it brought life to a standstill in parts of all the central United States. About 6 million people -- 20% of the U.S. population -- were under winter weather warnings, watches and advisories in the 750,000 square miles affected.

Drivers during these storms are encouraged to travel with survival kits in their cars just as people in earthquake prone regions should keep survival kits in their homes and cars. In a winter storm travelers often get stranded in their vehicles and need to know the six survival rules: Do not panic, remain in the vehicle, keep fresh air circulating to avoid the buildup of carbon monoxide, keep active by clapping hands and moving legs for circulation, keep dome light on so others can see you and the occupants in the car can be observed and lastly, do not allow all occupants in the vehicle to sleep at the same time.

While waiting for the snow plows to clear the roads it seemed like a good time as any to clean the attic. Claudia does this every winter when snow-bound. Storms were so massive the Kansas National

Guard would search the interstate and highways for any stranded travelers and all travel including flights was affected.

The single-detached, suburban home was deeply entrenched in snow, including the front and backyards. Being no stranger to this winter weather she had prepared for the worse (as she does every year); plenty of firewood, bottled water and food were stored.

Untying the twine and carefully opening the brown box she lifted the top and gazed upon the most beautiful red silk dress she'd ever seen. With amazement and wondering where it came from; she exhaled and smiled remembering her sister Katie mentioning the dress before she died two months ago (September). Fourth stage ovarian cancer sequestered her life while semi-conscious on an intravenous drip of morphine. Standing there she remembered Katie's muddled words, "…the silk dress…attic," and it still made no sense.

The phone was ringing and Claudia quickly covered the box, laid it aside and down the latter out the attic she went to answer it. She was expecting a call from her high school friend Sharon to get an idea of when she might get a flight into Kansas. With the current weather conditions it did not look promising; they might have to postpone this visit until the weather is more favorable for travel.

Sharon was hoping to help Claudia gather and bundle Katie's things to give to the Goodwill donation center. She also planned to assist her in returning the hospital bed, wheelchair, the multi-channel infusion pump and other equipment. The infusion pump was a customized drug library. With three independent fluid delivery channels and a drug dose calculator, it safely and quickly delivered infusion therapy for ambulatory and emergency room patients in the hospital and during air transport. Towards the end Katie was infused with morphine for pain to keep her comfortable and fluids for hydration.

Sharon thought they might take a trip to Florida and visit Disney World, Universal Studios Orlando or Lego Land. They were both big kids at heart and excited about exploring Florida's tourist attractions. The postponement was indefinite and Claudia was a smidgen disappointed, she'd looked forward to some vacation time and a change of pace.

THE ELITE RUNNER

Chapter Two

Two years Claudia's junior, Katie was athletic, health conscious, and an avid marathon runner. She seriously struggled running in the Boston Marathon, April 15, 2013, and barely finished thirty-minutes after the winner and other elite runners crossed the finish line. Severely exhausted and gasping to breathe she collapsed.

While training she'd noticed the increased struggle to complete her mileage which she scheduled according to the Boston Athletic Association (BAA). Training began the day after Thanksgiving 2012 and as a national competitor and for this marathon it involved several phases of varied running over a five month period. In February 2013, she became symptomatic but attributed it to the stomach flu she had two weeks after Halloween. She noticed it necessary to allow extra time for recovery from training workouts.

Katie was well aware physical training stresses the body, and during recovery it adapts. But without rest and recovery, there can be no adaptation. Her training spanned seven days a week for five months, which included scheduled days off or days of minimum exercise. It was important for her to recover completely from workouts so she could train hard when it was time to train hard; which could be every week, ten days, or every two weeks.

As an elite runner, her training for tempo running was seriously being challenged. She could not seem to overcome the discomfort in her abdomen.

Katie's training schedule was intense as it would be for any elite runner because she gauged her training by weekly mileage.

It's useful for getting an idea of the volume of training, but it is not the only measuring stick. How much one is training is a combination of volume and intensity. Katie never got hung up on logging a set number of weekly miles. If she has a day or two off she did not cram two days of training into one. She just picked up the program and continued because for her, lost days are simply lost.

Tempo running was an important factor in marathon training for Katie which is defined as + 10 seconds per mile from your projected marathon pace. If she was planning on running 26.2 miles at seven minutes per mile, she did lots of training at or near this pace. She knew this is one of the major differences between elite runners' marathon training and others training for the event.

Unlike most runners or joggers that are simply trying to finish the event in a halfway decent condition, as an elite runner she essentially viewed it as "racing" the event. This is why she attempted to run 26.2 miles at a pace faster than her every day run pace. Part of Katie's strategy was physiological. While nearly everyone else is training running marathons slower than their everyday pace, Katie knew through intense training her marathon race pace as an elite runner, would be a challenge.

To a large degree, Katie tried to simulate race conditions as much as possible during training. She did not go out and race a marathon daily, but realized every facet of the race needed to be practiced. The training program included tempo running toward the end of long runs and allowing her body to maintain her marathon race pace beyond twenty miles.

15 The Silk Dress

As an elite runner she also practiced water stops, drinking large volumes of water and/or carbohydrate solutions during training.

Other important things she considered were when training for a marathon such as Boston, downhill running was incorporated. Training at the time of the day the race starts and in the predicted weather conditions as much as possible were also useful. A "dress rehearsal" several weeks prior to the event was done in a race or long run. This time was also used to try out all racing clothing, shoes, socks, and pre-race meals. This was done far enough in advance to allow for changes to take place - and for any blisters to heal.

Her total warm up routine did not last for more than 15 minutes. She stretched her quads, hamstrings, Achilles tendons, calves, back, and the upper body. She stretched according to need, depending on soreness, tightness prior to the upcoming workout. For stretching she included warm-up for at least 5 minutes with light jogging; performed stretches in a controlled and smooth manner; held each stretch for at least 15-25 seconds; and, did not strain, bounce or force a stretch.

She was always ready to adjust and adapt a workout to the conditions. In New England the winter weather can vary from Arctic-like conditions to mild spring days. If it is an exceptionally poor day, then she adjusted the workout by cutting down the distance or intensity, decreased the number of reps, or increased the rest time. In cold weather she expected to run slower, have a higher heart rate, and feel worse than she would in good conditions.

Katie paid close attention to what her body told her. As an experienced runner she always listened to herself honestly. She could not ignore that the fatigued feeling was lasting more than several days in a row, so she scheduled in some rest and recovery time.

The historic Boston course would start on Main Street in the rural New England town of Hopkinton and follow Route 135 through Ashland, Framingham, Natick, and Wellesley to where Route 16 joins Route 135. It continues on Route 16 through Newton Lower Falls to Commonwealth Avenue, turning right at the fire station onto Commonwealth which is Route 30. The route continues on Commonwealth through the Newton Hills, bearing right at the reservoir onto Chestnut Hill Avenue to Cleveland Circle. The route then turns left onto Beacon Street continuing to Kenmore Square, and then follows Commonwealth Avenue inbound. There the course turns right onto Hereford Street (Note: against normal traffic flow) then left onto Boylston Street, finishing near the John Hancock Tower in Copley Square.

At the finish line, the marathon volunteers and emergency medical team could not revive Katie, her vitals were slow and pulse was weak. The onsite ambulance transported Katie to the Boston Medical Center. She'd crossed the finish line two hours after the winners finished the course; one-hour prior to the bombings. It was her worse time ever.

The elite women runners started the race at 9:30 a.m., and the elite men followed about 30 minutes later. About 27,000 runners were in the field for the Patriots' Day race. At the time of the explosions, approximately 17,000 runners had completed the race while 9,000 more were still advancing toward the finish line. The explosions occurred in the last 225 yards of the course, near a large number of spectators, resulting in 3 deaths and 264 people injured.

The scale of the incident required local, state, and federal partners to carry out a coordinated multi-agency response. Hospitals treated over 140 victims during the aftermath of the incident. All of these victims survived.

Claudia was walking through the den when she heard the "Special Report" regarding a Boston bombing on the KCTV5 News. She stopped and stared as she clutched her chest. The calls she'd made to Katie's cell earlier had all gone to voicemail. There is a one-hour time difference between Kansas and Boston and Claudia feared the worse.

Lelisa Desisa won the men's division with a time of 2:10:22. Rita Jeptoo won the women's division with a time of 2:26:25. More than $800,000 of prize money was awarded. Jeptoo is the third consecutive Kenyan winner. East Africans have won 17 of the past 19 races of the women's side.

Claudia knew Katie's running time and thought she should have made it across the finish line before the bombing. By now, three hours after the starting she should have heard from her. Friends and family were using all sources of social media to contact Claudia and Katie but five hours later there was still no response or news.

Thirty-minutes to it being six hours, Claudia received a call from Boston Memorial. After stabilizing Katie the hospital was inundated with the incoming injured from the bombing. Using her registration number they were able to identify her through the Boston Athletic Association; Claudia was Katie's emergency contact.

When the phone rang she jumped anxiously and as she answered the call she immediately became light-headed from prolonged anxiety and gripped the counter barstool to keep her balance. The caller identified themselves as Boston Medical Center and stated Katie was not affected by the bombing. Claudia began to cry tears of joy and the caller continued stating, she fainted as she crossed the finish line and they are running test to identify the cause. The hospital needed Katie's medical information to help them speed up the process. Claudia was able to provide them with insurance coverage, doctor's names and some health information. In the meantime, Claudia booked a 7:50 a.m. non-stop flight through Jet Blue Airlines to Logon International Airport in Boston to arrive 11:50 a.m. From there she took a cab to the medical center.

The cab driver was friendly and asked about her flight, the purpose of her trip and began talking about the bombing. The driver noticed that Claudia's eyes became teary as she searched for a tissue in her purse. From that point the driver was silent.

19 The Silk Dress

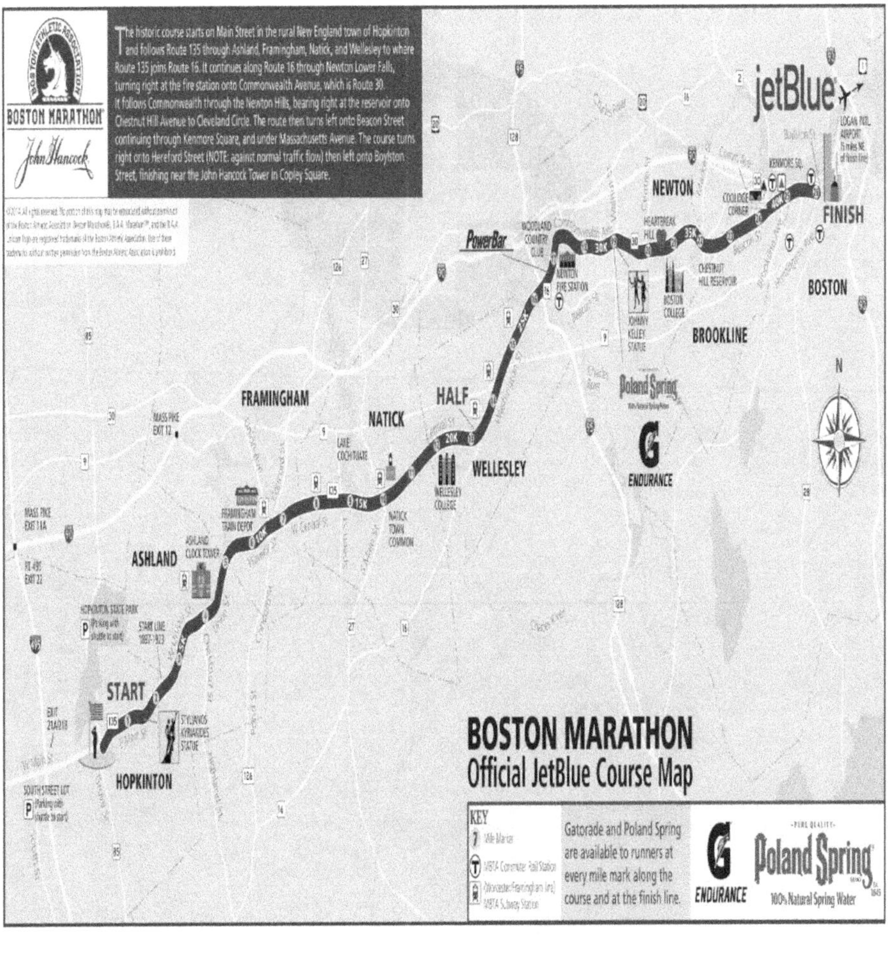

DAY AFTER YESTERDAY

Chapter Three

The Double Tree Hotel by Hilton was two miles from the hospital and one of the few reputable hotels with rooms available. Most were filled to capacity with no vacancies because of the marathon. The cabby took her to the Double Tree; she had him wait as she did an express check-in so her reservations would not be cancelled. She sent her carryon luggage to the room and rushed back to the cab to go straightway to Boston Medical Center. Traffic was horrendous due to the bombing and some of the marathon routes remained blocked for further investigation.

Katie had not been an actual victim of the bombing and Claudia had not thought much about its overall effect on the city. She paid the cabby and entered the hospital through the main lobby. People and families seemed to have camped overnight waiting for reports of their friends and loved ones. The information desk swarmed with people asking questions while the phones were ringing incessantly; people were coming and going emphatically. It was utter chaos.

Security officers were trying to manage the influx of people and the constant hustle and bustle. Fast forward was the pace and as she took it all in, things seemed to move in slow motion, as though she was in a different time or dimension. While Claudia turned gazing, working her way to the information desk the receptionist asked if she could help her. Claudia seemed preoccupied as the receptionist asked a second time. She gave the name of her sister and discovered she'd been moved from Intensive Care Unit (ICU) to the Step Down Unit (SDU) which provides an intermediate level of care between the (ICUs) and the general medical-surgical wards. These units, which are also commonly referred to as intermediate care unit and transitional care units, are found in many, but not all, hospitals in developed nations. Typically, these units are staffed at a higher nurse to patient ratio than general medical-surgical wards but not as high as ICUs. Katie was assigned to room 462-A. The elevators were packed with people going in each direction. After twenty-minutes or so, Claudia was able to get to the fourth floor.

Katie was sedated and connected to pumps, tubes and all sorts of medical apparatus. The marathon clothing and her signature Brooks Unisex Racer ST-5 running shoes were crumpled into the hospital belongings bag that sat on the small cabinet next to her bed. Exhausted, Claudia softly touched Katie's arm while resting her own head in her other hand as she sat next to the bed.

The attending physician, Dr. Raven Hillary entered, introduced himself and said she was waiting on the test results to confirm her preliminary prognosis. Since Katie was stable, she suggested Claudia grab something to eat, get some rest and return tomorrow and they would have the results by 10:00 a.m. Hospital staff at the nurse's station suggested she try Mike's City Diner, it's in walking distance, not too pricey and they serve breakfast, lunch and dinner, including home style burgers and sandwiches. Claudia ordered something from the "lite" menu and returned to her hotel.

The hot shower was rejuvenating and relaxing; she was exhausted physically and emotionally. Just before falling asleep she plugged her Galaxy phone to the charger and then into the outlet and set the alarm for 7:00 a.m. Every station on the television was reporting the bombing and its devastation. Area surveillance cameras, the locations of the blasts along with other intelligence information rendered two suspects. Her mind quickly succumbed to the call of sleep.

When she woke to the sound of the alarm she slowly got out of bed. The temperature the day of the marathon was in the upper 40s °F (8–10 °C) range and climbed to 54 °F (12 °C) at the finish. She wore a pink and grey sweat suit with matching tennis shoes.
The hotel offered a free continental breakfast she grabbed a caramel cappuccino, diced seasonal fresh fruit and a blueberry muffin then hailed a cab and returned to Boston Memorial.

+HOSPITAL
HOSPITAL

MEDICAL ASSESSMENT

Chapter Four

Epithelial ovarian cancers, the most common type, arise from the surface of the ovary, and are typically seen in women over the age of 50. While epithelial ovarian cancer has been called "the silent disease" for its lack of symptoms, more recent evidence indicates that several signs may develop which could be suggestive of this disease. As Katie researched her symptoms she crossed a national consensus statement of ovarian cancer symptoms which included:

- Bloating
- Pelvic or abdominal pain
- Difficulty eating or feeling full quickly
- Urinary symptoms, such as urgency or frequency

The reports stated these symptoms are more likely to occur in women with ovarian cancer than in the general population, and are persistent and progressive over a short period of time. Most importantly, the symptoms typically represent a distinctive change from normal. Development of these symptoms and the decline in her running ability prompted Katie to consult with her health care provider to order a screening evaluation for potential ovarian cancer.

Katie learned a lot during her research, in particularly the risk factors. Several risk factors are known to increase the likelihood for ovarian cancer development. These include:

- Genetic predisposition through deleterious mutations, Family history of breast and/or ovarian cancer, especially in a mother, daughter, or sister.
- Age over 55 years
- Never having had children

Although Katie did not have children and was not over 55 she was experiencing the symptoms. Neither sister knew much about the family's medical history, especially concerning the women in their family because she and Claudia were both adopted. Since the marathon was two weeks away she scheduled the evaluation the week after.

Her health care provider had insisted she schedule a screening appointment within the week and testing be done immediately but Katie wanted to wait until after the marathon. Her doctor reluctantly scheduled a comprehensive medical history and scheduled a physical exam, including examination of the pelvis with rectal exam. Additionally, testing included imaging studies of the pelvis (and abdomen) via ultrasonography (US) and a computed tomography (CT). Trans-vaginal ultrasonography which utilizes high-frequency sound waves is typically the best way to identify growths and cysts on the ovary. CT imaging, which involves a series of computerized x-rays, can identify masses outside of the ovaries and in the abdomen suggestive of the spread of cancer.

Upon Katie's arrival to the Boston Medical Center and after she was stabilized the ER doctor, after retrieving information from Claudia and other sources reviewed her medical information including the recent scheduling of tests from her gynecologist.

27 The Silk Dress

There was also a referral for a new blood test, called HE4, which is used to determine the likelihood of ovarian cancer.

These test in addition to OVA1 test, prompted the ER doctor to refer Katie to a gynecologic oncologist for further evaluation. After the test was run it would be discovered the suspected diagnosis was cancer and blood would be drawn to measure levels of a specific protein known as CA-125. While ovarian cancer cells produce this protein, women with small cancers confined to the ovary may not show any elevation in blood tests. Furthermore, elevated levels are seen with a variety of benign and normal conditions, such as fibroids, endometriosis, simple ovarian cysts, as well as gastritis, hepatitis, and diverticulitis and are usually seen in women over 55 years of age.

Katie fainted as she crossed the finished line at 2:05 p.m. due to acute dehydration, fatigue and the accelerating symptoms of ovarian cancer. By the time she was coherent enough to interview the hospital had already contacted her sister. The staff decided to wait for Claudia's arrival before giving Katie the diagnostic results.

Due to the recent bombing the atmosphere in the medical center was still very much chaotic. People were frantically awaiting results and information regarding relatives and friends injured in the bombing. News broadcast were reporting three were killed and more than 141 were injured. An 8-year-old boy was listed amongst the dead. The Boston Globe reported, citing law enforcement sources briefed on the investigation among the injured, 17 were reported in critical condition. The victims at eight local hospitals were as young as two. There were so many people in that area that they couldn't get ambulances in there, people were being transported out in wheelchairs. One spectator reported one guy had no legs the bones were just sticking out, a horrible sight.

Massachusetts General Hospital was treating 19 victims, and six were in surgery in critical condition, four suffering "traumatic amputations" from having legs cut off by the force of the explosions. Tufts Medical Center had nine patients and we're expecting more. Brigham and Women's Hospital reported receiving 18 to 20 injured from the explosions, two in critical condition. As night fell at Brigham and Women's Hospital, a Level One trauma center, three police officers with rifles stood guard at the front entrance. Inside, physicians cared for 28 victims of the Boylston Street blast, including two in critical condition, two at risk of losing limbs and nine who needed surgery.

Boston's trauma centers were praised and applauded for saving dozens of Marathon bombing victims, treating one person after another who arrived at their doors with limbs torn off or mangled, and some patients having lost most of their blood.

In particular, the bombings brought forward a problem that has been problematic for trauma hospitals for years: the identification of victims.

Within minutes of the April 15 bombing, many patients arrived unconscious and without purses, wallets, or family members to identify them. An ambulance brought one woman to Massachusetts General Hospital with a handbag, but it wasn't hers. It belonged to her best friend, who was killed on Boylston Street. Before the mix up was noticed, the family of the dead woman was told she was in a hospital bed.

29 The Silk Dress

There were challenges keeping patients straight at Brigham and Women's Hospital, too. Staff assigned unidentified victims six-digit numbers, but they were confusing, and doctors and nurses had to continually double-check that imaging test results and medications were going to the correct patient. One ER doctor stated that fortunately there were no mix-ups, but there were certainly some near misses.

Relatives and friends crowded waiting rooms, desperately searching for loved ones and pleading for any shred of information about their conditions. It didn't help that siblings and spouses had been separated and that wounded parents and children too, had been rushed to different hospitals.

A mother at Boston Medical Center, where her daughter-in-law was being treated, anxiously searched for her son. Eventually, a hospital administrator called over to Beth Israel Deaconess Medical Center and located the son.

Hospital staff was alerted to the bombings when a physician at the scene sent a tweet. The message was picked up by an anesthesiologist, who suggested that the hospital postpone all elective surgery. Patients began arriving by car, police van, and ambulance to a full emergency department at 3:04 p.m.

The first six victims were wheeled to emergency surgery; only one had been identified and she was near death. There was no measurable blood pressure; she had lost all of her blood and was very critical. An extra couple of minutes and she wouldn't have survived. She was lucky.

Those with identification were mixed up with others that did not have identification. If a Driver's license was found in a purse the picture ID did not match, or the patient was too mangle or loss too much blood to safely conclude identity. Everything was happening at a fast forward pace.

Some of the dead were mistaken for the living and the living for the dead. It was an unfortunate mix up and hospital administrators in the midst of the chaos were trying to strategize the prevention of identification errors. They were in the middle of a catastrophic crisis trying to save life. Reconnecting patients and families was challenging throughout the city.

Boston Medical Center had its share of trauma patients. An ER nurse handed a patient advocacy worker a Post-it note with the name of an injured man and his wife's name and marathon race number. This was the method used to identify Katie.

At some hospitals after the first few patients' arrival others poured in by groves in the first 30 minutes. This arrival rate of patients and the magnitude of the injuries overwhelmed any hospital's standard registration services. The patients needed immediate medical attention and it was taking too long to get them into the computers. They soon found that the strategy of assigning everyone a six-digit number resolved in creating its own headaches.

If anything good can be focused on from this horrific attack, trauma doctors surmised Boston was fortunate that the bombs exploded at an event where dozens of medical and public safety personnel already were stationed, and at an hour when shifts changed at the hospitals, nearly doubling the number of medical staff on site.

31 The Silk Dress

From worms to silk…

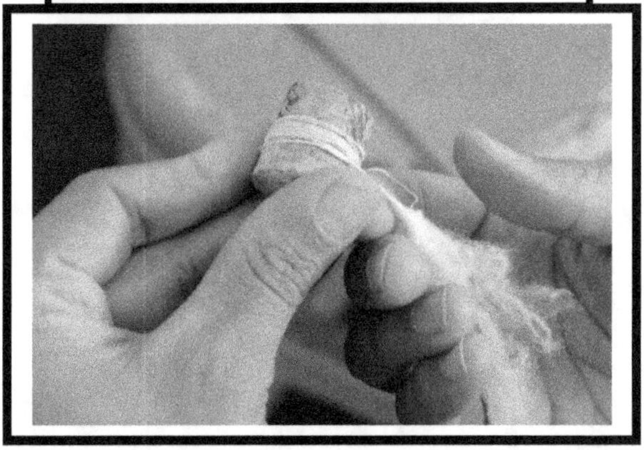

絲

ACME IMPORTED SILK FASHIONS
输入性的ACME丝绸FASHIONS

Chapter Five

For the annual Christmas party Katie ordered a beautiful silk dress online from AIS Fashions for $106 plus shipping. She did not care for shopping and online was the shopping way-to-go for her for some time now. She wanted to look fabulous at this party because her former fiancé was expected to be there.

When she opened the box it was breathtaking. The color was like no red she had ever seen, so intense it appeared liquescent. As she slipped it over her head to try it on, instantly it formed to her body…giving the perfect fit…as if it were tailored specifically for her.

Gazing at herself in the mirror she was captivated by her own image. It was though someone else besides her was standing there and immediately she felt a sudden change in her body. She was mesmerized and could not take it off because the dress captivated her in such a way it seemed controlling. She smiled and thought she will be stunning, the "best dressed" for sure. After thirty-minutes (which seemed like five minutes) the dress was placed on a hanger and she felt a slight twinge in her abdomen.

The dress was crafted from ancient Chinese silk that was connected to the mystical Gu silkworm. This was a powerful venom-based poison associated with cultures of south China, particularly Nanyue. The traditional preparation of gu poison involved sealing several venomous creatures (e.g., centipede, snake, and scorpion) into a closed utensil, where they devoured one another and allegedly concentrated their toxins into a single survivor. Gu was used in black magic practices such as manipulating sexual partners, creating malignant diseases, and causing death.

According to Chinese folklore, a *gu* spirit could transform into various animals, typically a worm, caterpillar, snake, frog, dog, or pig.

There is a second *gu* known as a "wug." It is an "anciently recorded type of artificially cultured poisonous creature, the survivor of several venomous creatures enclosed in a container, and transformed into a type of demon or spirit.

The *Zhouli* ritual text describes a Shushi official who was charged with the duty of exterminating poisonous *gu*, attacking it with spells and thus exorcising it, as also with the duty of attacking it with efficacious herbs. All persons ingesting *gu* was controlled and employed according to the demonic needs. A commentary explains "poisonous *gu*" as "wugs" that cause sickness in people.

As the legal measures of individual dynasties demonstrate, administrative officials viewed gu as a reality, as late as the nineteenth century. The primary host was considered a criminal; a person guilty of the despicable act of preparing and administering gu poison was executed, occasionally with his entire family, in a gruesome manner.

In addition to the obvious desire to punish severely criminal practices that could result in the death of the victim, it is possible that Confucian distaste for the accumulation of material goods, and above all for the resulting social mobility, contributed to this attitude. Indeed, the penalties of the use of gu poison appear to have been more severe than those for other forms of murder.

Silk making is intriguing and begins with the adult silk moth, which is raised solely for reproduction. Batches of moths are kept in special houses where temperature, light and air are controlled by brazier air vents, and blinds. This is to control reproduction so that the moths in each batch will mate at the same time. Since the moths' lives are controlled to insure mating occurs at the same time, the eggs also are produced and hatched at roughly the same time. Once the silkworms hatch from their eggs, they are kept on bamboo trays and fed fresh mulberry leaves to store fat while they mature. As the silkworms mature, they spin cocoons from a jellylike substance in their silk glands. After about a week, some cocoons are steamed or baked to kill the worms inside. Some of the cocoons are left to nurture and release moths to reproduce. The cocoons are then plunged into boiling water to unravel the silky fibers. each cocoon consists of a thread about half a mile long. Once the cocoon fibers are unraveled, several are reeled together on a spool to make a thread strong enough for spinning. The fine silk fibers are woven into different types of cloth, from filmy gauze to heavy brocades.

The dress Katie ordered had a silent history that no one ever discovered. It held the curse of the Gu silkworm. It was first fashioned in the 160's for a Chinese Emperor's wife as a gift. She wore it to an ancient celebration and died three weeks later of a painful, agonizing illness.

As centuries past it adapts itself to that era's fashion and claims the life of whoever wears it.

Because it is demon inspired and influenced from the spirit of darkness it manifests itself year after year.

Katie was extraordinarily beautiful in the red silk dress. It not only transformed her but captivated everyone who saw her, especially the men. Its demonic power caused them to desire her, even those who never really noticed her before. Jealousy, speculation, accusations and more were the argumentative conversation of every couple the night of, and next morning after the party. Those possessed by the dress usually realize something is off kilter the next morning but by then it is too late.

Katie was indeed more than fairytale beautiful. The dress gave the illusion and appearance of voluptuous curves all in the right places. She seemed as perfect as a Barbie doll and most desirable. Most certainly she was the life of the party…a goddess. Every man danced with her whether he was escorting someone or. The ex-finance' was having second thoughts and wanted to rekindle their romance. But to Katie, it seemed she was mesmerized or spellbound because none of the men interested her, it was the ability to allure and attract their passion that excited her. She could have slept with all and every man there had she desired.

Their physical and emotional reaction to her was the intrigue.

37 The Silk Dress

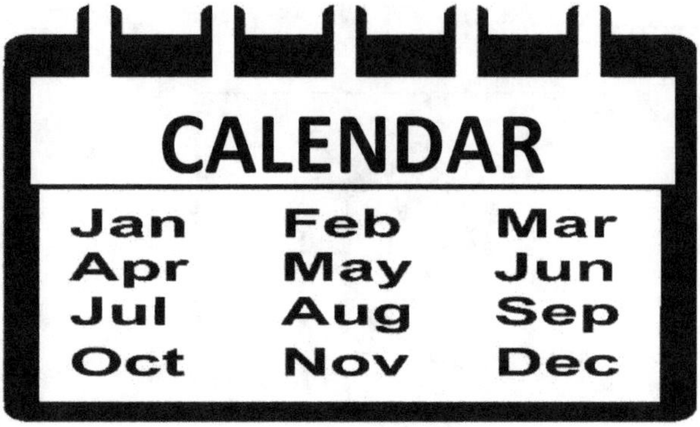
CALENDAR
Jan Feb Mar
Apr May Jun
Jul Aug Sep
Oct Nov Dec

ONE HUNDRED THIRTY-TWO DAYS

Chapter Six

Delicately Dr. Hilary shared with Claudia what to expect towards Katie's end of life. She suggested palliative team care over hospice. It's fairly new and has its own distinct mission: to relieve suffering and improve quality of life for people with serious illnesses. Hospice is usually done in the home or in a skilled nursing facility. Claudia opted to take her home with palliative care because the insurance would provide all of the necessary durable medical equipment, medications and a palliative care team to help her through the process.

Hospice programs far outnumber palliative care programs. Generally, once enrolled through a referral from the primary care physician, a patient's hospice care program, which is overseen by a team of hospice professionals, is administered in the home. Hospice often relies upon the family caregiver, as well as a visiting hospice nurse. While hospice can provide round-the-clock care in a nursing home, a specially equipped hospice facility, or, on occasion, in a hospital, this is not the norm.

Reading literature given to her by Katie's doctor Claudia learned when asked about dying, most people say they want a peaceful and pain free death. Contrary to myths and horror stories this is usually possible with the right care and treatment. It makes the thought of death far less frightening. The medical team will make every effort to control any symptoms and keep the patient as comfortable as possible. The palliative care team offers relief, support, and comfort to patients and their family and friends. It involves caring for the physical, emotional, psychological, and spiritual needs in the best way possible. The palliative care team usually consists of specialists including nurses, social workers, volunteers, pastoral care workers, (if you so desire) and other health care professionals. Others included as part of the team are dieticians, physiotherapists and counsellors. One of Claudia's major concerns was pain control. She did not want it controlled with distressing side-effects or unmanageable addiction to the pain relievers.

Dr. Hillary also explained other symptoms Katie may experience such as: Loss of appetite, loss of weight, fatigue, confusion, and restlessness were a few. Towards the end of her life there may be some noticeable physical changes in the patient because the body begins its natural process of slowing down all its functions. How long this takes varies from person to person - it may take hours or days. The dying person will feel weak and sleep a lot. When death is very near the dying person may have sleepiness and difficulty waking (semi-conscious), difficulty swallowing or not wanting to eat or drink at all, loss of control of bladder and bowel control, restless movements (as though in pain), changes in breathing, noisy breathing, cold feet, hands, legs and arms, confusion and disorientation, and complete loss of consciousness.

She had signed a "**do not resuscitate**" directive which was kept in her records. This was a relief for Claudia; she would not have to make that decision. From Dr. Hilary's experience she estimated 6 months for Katie. Claudia made all the arrangements to bring Katie home so she could die with dignity and receive the best of care.

41 The Silk Dress

Claudia never thought much about death and dying but the team and physician were very helpful and did what they could to help her prepare.

Some people may seem more at peace as death gets closer while others may become very anxious, fearful or angry. Some people may appear to withdraw even from the people they love and care about. But this doesn't mean that they don't care anymore. These events are all very normal and a natural part of dying.

Even if the physical body is ready to shut down, some people may resist death. They may still have issues they want to resolve or relationships they want to put right. Claudia understood it was important to understand these things and to let Katie know she was there for her to help her with any of these issues.

The team helped her also understand she was likely to feel some very strong emotions while waiting during the end of days. She may feel that she wants to try and change what is happening but often all she can do is give a lot of support and comfort during this difficult time while allow her to share any memories or feelings she might have. Because some people will hold on until they receive assurance Claudia wanted Katie to know it was all right to let go and die whenever she was ready. Some people will hold on until they have heard these words from the people they love. So letting them go can be one of the most important and loving things we can do for them.

Katie lived six months and two days after she was brought to her sister's home. Only a few times towards her end of days were she conscious but she and Claudia were able to talk about what had transpired over the last few months. Katie smiled when she learned she had completed the marathon. Her last week or so she was mostly semi-conscious, and no longer eating or drinking.

During their few conversations, while she was lucid, Katie tried to discuss and share her experience with the red silk dress but nothing she said made much sense to Claudia. She actually thought the medications were the cause and she would probably give the dress to the Salvation Army along with the rest of her belongings.

Her departure was peaceful and quick. Breathing patterns began to change and there were periods of shallow and deep breathing, alternating over short periods of time. She actually seemed to stop breathing for as long as ten to twenty seconds before beginning again. Twenty seconds may not sound like a very long time, but it certainly seems so in this situation. It was long enough that she mistakenly thought the end had come and gone but was startled to hear Katie take a sudden deep breath. The breathing changes had Claudia feeling Katie was experiencing discomfort, but the team nurse assured her it was actually normal and not a sign of distress.

She remembered the literature on death and the palliative team saying there might be a rattling noise (often referred to as the "death rattle." Its medical name is terminal respiratory secretions coming from the back of the throat because they lose the ability to cough or swallow.

Katie was gone. The breathing stopped, her heart stopped beating, her body color became pale, she became cool to the touch and her muscles relaxed.

43 The Silk Dress

Claudia's emotions seemed to float aimlessly. She was sad and relieved at the same time. Sad because she loved and would miss her sister; relieved because Katie no longer had to suffer. The time of death was called and recorded, mortuary was called to retrieve the remains and viewing clothing was given to attendants.

THE FINAL CHAPTER

Chapter Seven

The services were held in Kansas City at the McGinley Hill Chapel and Mortuary. Just a few close friends and Claudia were in attendance. Due to excessive weight loss the service was closed casket with a beautiful 16 x 20 portrait of Katie in a beautiful red, silk dress sitting on an easel next to the casket. It was a memorable and beautiful service. Katie's obituary read interestingly and as intriguingly as she was.

The music was a CD of Katie's favorites played before and during the services. Bette Midler's "Wind Beneath My Wings," Elton John's "Circle of Life," Burt Bacharach and Carole Bayer Sager's, "That's What Friends Are For." An option offered by the mortuary was hosting the repast and Claudia was really happy she opted for that after the services. After mingling, and receiving condolences from friends she was physically and emotionally exhausted.

When she returned home she was happy that all of the hospital equipment had been returned. The following morning Claudia took the hospital belongings bag up to the attic and placed it among other memorabilia. As she sat on the floor amongst the attic's relics and vestiges she reflected on the red silk dress and opened the box one more time. Not knowing what to do she decided to research the company where it was purchased and found there was not now nor, was there ever a record of the ACME Imported Silk company in the United States or anywhere in the world.

The computer search and events leading to Katie's illness, death and memorial had taken its toll. Maybe later she would investigate the mystery around the silk dress but for now she desperately needed to give her mind and body a rest. The dress sat in the box collecting dust until winter. She placed it amongst a pile of leftover things she would later give to the Salvation Army.

Before the first snowfall, Claudia packed her car with Katie's belongings along with a few other attic memorabilia and drove to the nearest Salvation Army center. The dress was donated in its original cardboard box. While rustling in her purse putting the receipt away her head panged.

Two weeks prior, while rumbling in the attic, gathering all the items to be donated she tried on the dress. After yanking off the sheet covering the wood-framed double sided, full length mirror; as she gazed the reflection was astonishing. The most beautiful being she'd ever seen. As Claudia stared at the flawless body and features she was transfixed on the being in the mirror. The downstairs clock chimed, startling her at half past the hour and she quickly removed the dress. The pangs in her head have increased with intensity daily.

Bibliography

Boston Marathon, Wikipedia, the free encyclopedia, April 15, 2013

Boston Athletic Association,

Boston Marathon 20213, Route Map, SB Nation

Boston Marathon, Elite Runner

Curse of the Gu Silk Worm, Wikipedia, the free encyclopedia

Cancer ResearchUK.Org

Fiction - Wikipedia, the free encyclopedia

Kansas City Transportation Department, 511 Winter Storm Survival.org

www.CaregiversLibrary.org

About the Author

Shiela Y. Harris...

...Is generally a writer of Christian subject matter with an astute knowledge of the Word with an intense and vast imagination. After publishing several Christian-based books she wrote two fictional works. Ms. Harris realizes she might be criticized by the staunched saints for the fiction but her major concern is not offending or dishonoring God.

Unfortunately, witchcraft is real and she is careful not to glorify or elevate it with God. Moreover, she enjoys releasing and bridling her imagination simultaneously.

Each of her works is entertaining, informative and brief reads. She encourages her readers to enjoy both genres and be the judge.

THE

END

OR IS IT?

www.ingramcontent.com/pod-product-compliance
Lightning Source LLC
Chambersburg PA
CBHW071317200626
46813CB00015B/2252
* 9 7 8 0 9 6 7 9 3 1 2 9 6 *